Hey, Little Ant

Phillip and Hannah Hoose

Illustrations by Debbie Tilley

TRICYCLE PRESS
Berkeley, California

KID: Hey, little ant down in the crack,

Can you hear me? Can you talk back?

See my shoe, can you see that?

Well, now it's gonna **squish** you flat!

ANT: Please, oh please, do not squish me,
Change your mind and let me be,
I'm on my way with a crumb of pie,
Please, oh **please**, don't make me die!

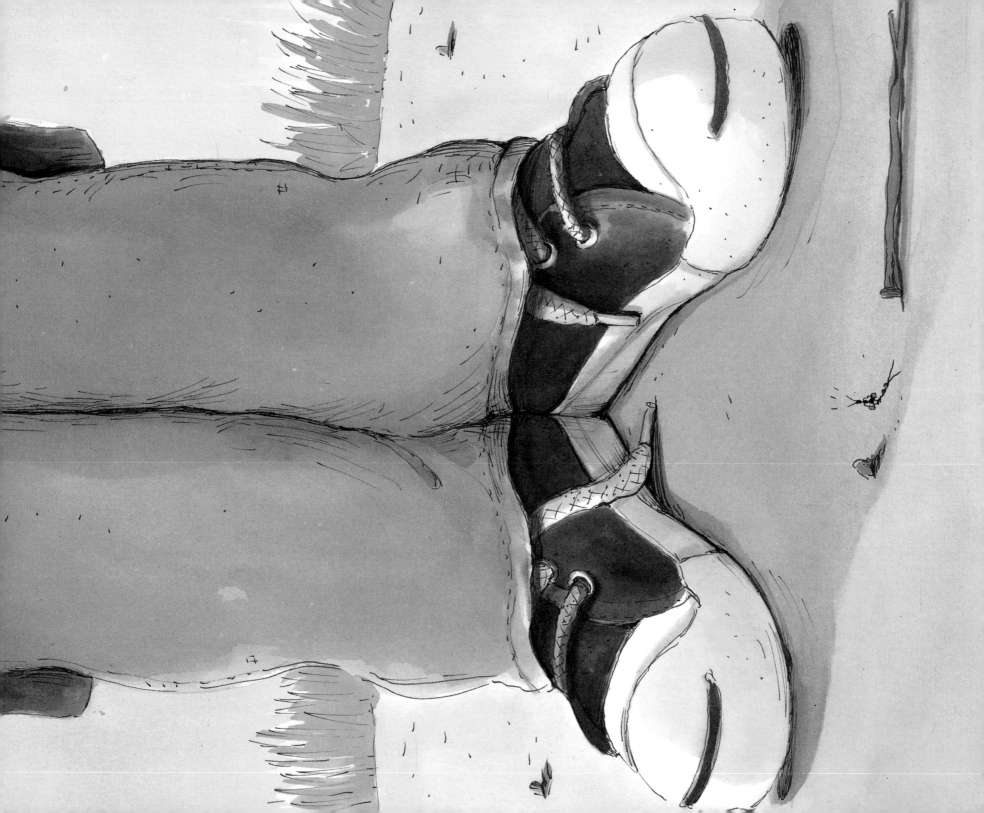

ANT: But you are a giant and giants can't
know how it feels to be an ant.
Come down close, I think you'll see
That you are very much like me.

KID: Are you crazy? **Me** like **you**?

I have a home and a family, too.

You're just a speck that runs around,
No one would care if my foot came down.

KID: But my mom says that ants are rude,

They carry off our picnic food!

They steal our chips and bread crumbs, too,

It's **good** if I squish a crook like you.

ANT: Hey, I'm not a crook, kid, read my lips!
Sometimes ants need crumbs and chips.
One little chip can feed my town,
So please don't make your shoe come down.

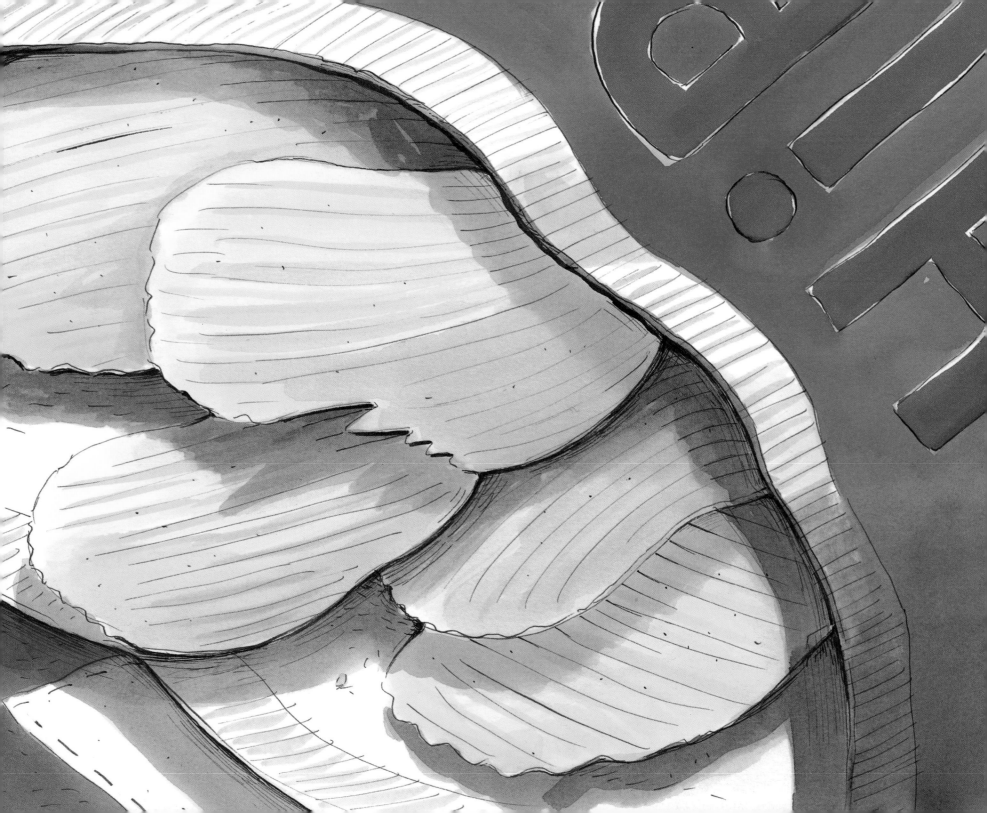

KID: But all my friends squish ants each day,
Squishing ants is a game we play.

YEAH

They're looking at me—they're listening, too.
They all say I **should** squish you.

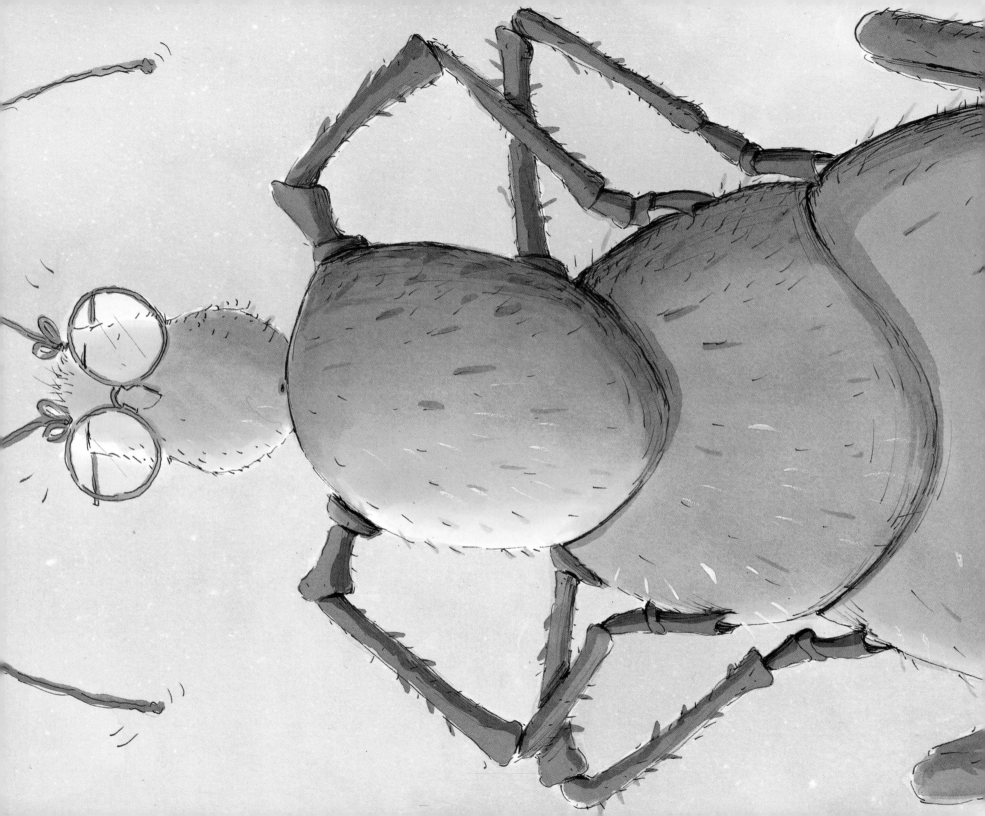

ANT: I can see you're big and strong,

Decide for yourself what's

right and wrong,

If you were me and I were you,

What would **you** want **me** to do?

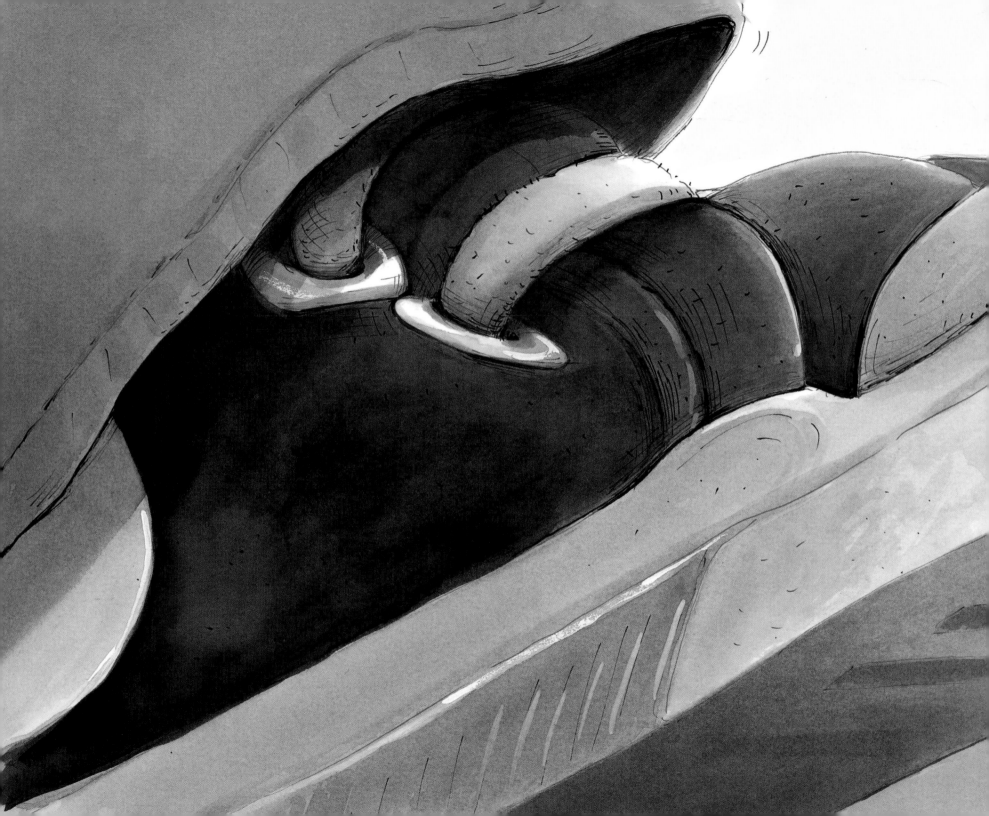

Should the ant get squished? Should the ant go free?

It's up to the kid, not up to me.

We'll leave the kid with the raised-up shoe.

What do you think that kid should do?

1. **KID:** Hey, little ant down in the crack,
Can you hear me? Can you talk back?
See my shoe, can you see that?
Well now it's gonna **squish** you flat!

2. **ANT:** Please, oh please, do not squish me,
Change your mind and let me be,
I'm on my way with a crumb of pie,
Please, oh **please,** don't make me die!

3. **KID:** Anyone knows that ants can't feel.
You're so tiny you don't look real.
I'm so big and you're so small,
I don't think it'll hurt at all.

4. **ANT:** But you are a giant and giants can't
Know how it feels to be an ant.
Come down close, I think you'll see
That you are very much like me.

5. **KID:** Are you crazy? **Me** like **you**?
I have a home and a family, too.
You're just a speck that runs around,
No one would care if my foot came down.

6. **ANT:** Oh big friend, you are so wrong,
My nest mates need me 'cause I am strong.
I dig our nest and feed baby ants, too,
I must not die beneath your shoe.

7. **KID:** But my mom says that ants are rude,
They carry off our picnic food!
They steal our chips and bread crumbs, too,
It's **good** if I squish a crook like you.

8. **ANT:** Hey, I'm not a crook, kid, read my lips!
Sometimes ants need crumbs and chips.
One little chip can feed my town,
So please don't make your shoe come down.

9. **KID:** But all my friends squish ants each day,
Squishing ants is a game we play.
They're looking at me—they're listening, too.
They all say I **should** squish you.

10. **ANT:** I can see you're big and strong,
Decide for yourself what's right and wrong,
If you were me and I were you,
What would **you** want **me** to do?

11. Should the ant get squished? Should the ant go free?
It's up to the kid, not up to me.
We'll leave the kid with the raised-up shoe.
What do you think that kid should do?

To all squished ants. –H.H.

To Ruby with the raised-up shoe. –P.H.

To Ian and his family, with special thanks
to Eric for his Hey, Little Centipede idea. –D.T.

Text copyright © 1998 by Phillip and Hannah Hoose
Illustrations copyright © 1998 by Debbie Tilley
Music copyright © 1992 by Precious Pie Music, Inc., BMI

Music and words © Precious Pie Music. A recorded version of *Hey, Little Ant* is available.
For ordering information, visit www.heylittleant.com.

TRICYCLE PRESS
a little division of Ten Speed Press
P.O. Box 7123
Berkeley, California 94707
www.tenspeed.com

Free *Hey, Little Ant Teachers' Guide* available on our Web site.
Book design by Susan Van Horn

Library of Congress Cataloging-in-Publication Data
Hoose, Phillip M., 1947–
Hey little ant / Phillip M. Hoose and Hannah Hoose ; illustrations by Debbie Tilley.   p. cm.
Summary: A song in which an ant pleads with the kid who is tempted to squish it.
ISBN 1-883672-54-6
1. Children's songs—Texts. [1. Ants—Songs and music. 2. Songs.] I. Hoose, Hannah.   II. Tilley, Debbie, ill.   III. Title.
PZ8.3.H774Hg 1998   782.42164'0268—dc21   [E]
98-14025

First printing, 1998
Printed in Hong Kong

9 10 11 12 — 06 05 04 03 02